BEAR's PICTURE

Story and pictures by
DANIEL PINKWATER

E. P. Dutton / New York

First published in 1972 by Holt, Rinehart and Winston.
Reissued in 1984 by E. P. Dutton.

Copyright © 1972 by Daniel Pinkwater

Published in the United States by E. P. Dutton, Inc.,
2 Park Avenue, New York, N.Y. 10016

Published simultaneously in Canada by
Fitzhenry & Whiteside Limited, Toronto

Printed in Hong Kong by South China Printing Co.
COBE   10 9 8 7 6 5 4 3 2 1

ISBN: 0-525-44102-6

For David Nyvall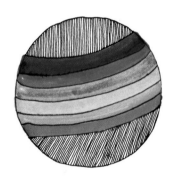

A bear wanted to paint a picture.

First he made an orange squiggle.

Then he had a look at it.

"I believe it wants some blue," said the bear. And he painted some blue.

Then the bear saw a rainbow and put that in too.

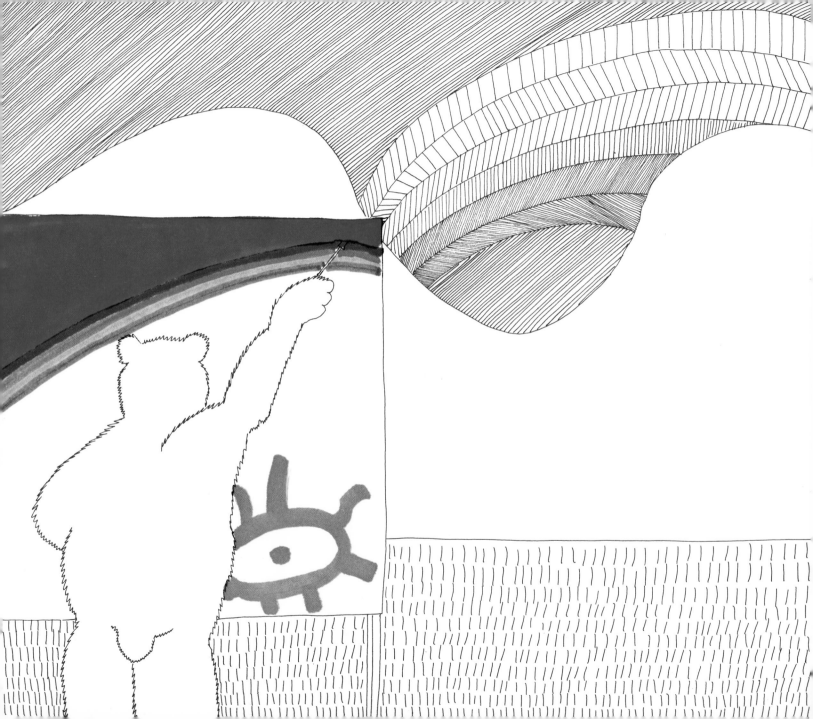

Two fine, proper gentlemen, out for a walk, came upon the bear.

"Look here," said the first fine, proper gentleman, "a bear painting a picture."

"Bears can't paint pictures," said the second fine, proper gentleman.

"Why not? Why can't a bear do anything he likes?" asked the bear.

"Because …" said the first fine, proper gentleman.

"Because …" said the second fine, proper gentleman.

"Bears aren't the sort of fellows who can do whatever they like," they both said together.

"Besides," said the first fine, proper gentleman, "that is a silly picture."

"Nobody can tell what it is supposed to be," said the second fine, proper gentleman.

"I can tell," said the bear, adding some green splotches.

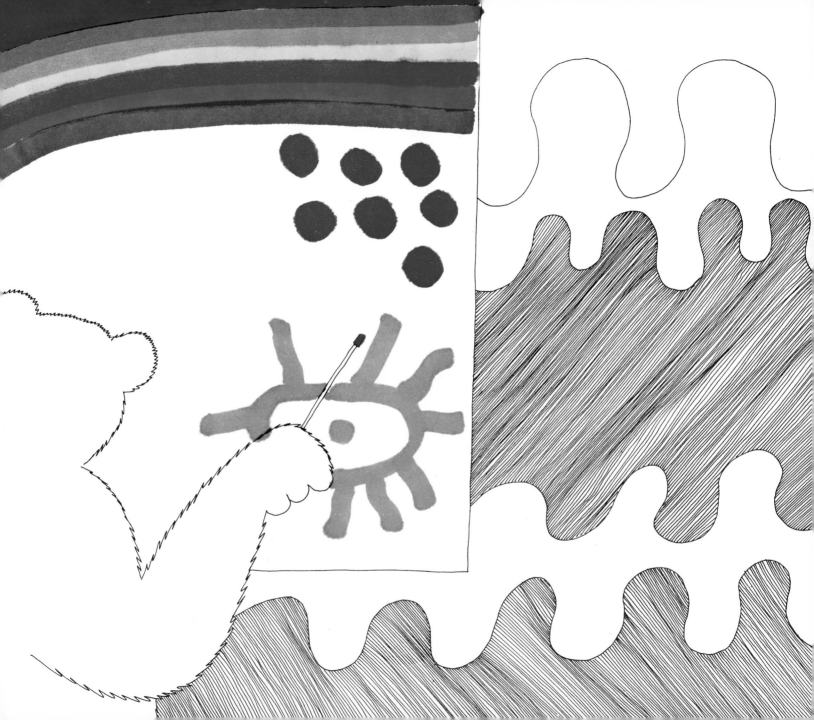

"Oh," said the first fine, proper gentleman.
"Oh," said the second fine, proper gentleman.
"Is it a butterfly? It looks a little like a butterfly."

"No," said the bear, mixing just the right kind of yellow. "It is not a butterfly."

"Ah," said the first fine, proper gentleman.
"Ah," said the second fine, proper gentleman.
"Is it a clown? It looks a little like a clown."

"No," said the bear, putting in some purple parts. "It is not a clown."

"Then what is it a picture of?" shouted the first and second fine, proper gentlemen together.

"It is a honey tree," said the bear. "It is a cold stream in the forest. It is a hollow log filled with soft leaves for a bear to keep warm in all winter long. It is a sunny day and a field full of flowers."

"It doesn't look like any of those to us," said the two fine, proper gentlemen.

"It doesn't have to," said the bear,
"it is *my* picture."

The two fine, proper gentlemen went away saying,
"Bears are not the sort of fellows to paint pictures."

But the bear looked at
his picture and was happy.